38538 00022 0058

P9-DNE-206

E
STEVENSON, James
Worse than the worst

DATE DUE

DEMCO, INC. 38-2931

James Stevenson

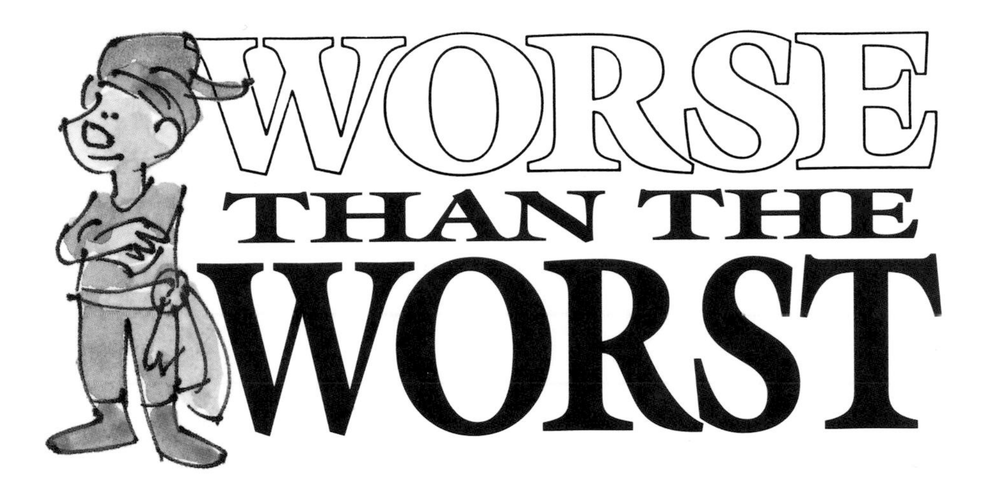

Greenwillow Books, New York

Watercolor paints and a black pen were used for the full-color art. The text type is Zapf International ITC.

Copyright © 1994 by James Stevenson

All rights reserved. No part of this book may be reproduced or utilized in any form or by any means, electronic or mechanical, including photocopying, recording, or by any information storage and retrieval system, without permission in writing from the Publisher, Greenwillow Books, a division of William Morrow & Company, Inc., 1350 Avenue of the Americas, New York, NY 10019.

Printed in Hong Kong by South China Printing Company (1988) Ltd.

First Edition 10 9 8 7 6 5 4 3 2 1

LIBRARY OF CONGRESS CATALOGING-IN-PUBLICATION DATA

Stevenson, James (date)
Worse than the worst / by James Stevenson.
p. cm.
Summary: When he comes for a brief visit, Warren proves to be just as difficult to get along with as his great-uncle Worst.
ISBN 0-688-12249-3 (trade).
ISBN 0-688-12250-7 (lib. bdg.)
[1. Behavior—Fiction. 2. Great-uncles—Fiction.]
I. Title.
PZ7.S84748Wv 1994
[E]—dc20 93-239 CIP AC

When the worst person in the world got up in the morning, it was sleeting and there was deep snow.

"Cars must be sliding off the road, people slipping on sidewalks, that kind of thing," said the worst.

33680
5-18-94

He made himself a bowl of dried figs. Daisy watched him. "No breakfast for you till you've gone out," he said to Daisy. "You know the rules."

Daisy pushed open the dog door and looked at all the snow.

"Go on," said the worst. "Don't be a wimp."

A few moments later Daisy stuck her head back in. She was shivering.

"Go away," said the worst. "You're letting cold wind in here."

There was a knock at the front door. It was the mail carrier.

"L-letter for you, Mr. Worst," he said.

"Why didn't you put it in my mailbox down on the road the way you're supposed to?" said the worst.

"Your m-mailbox is r-rusted shut," said the mail carrier.

"Don't get my porch all snowy," said the worst, and slammed the door.

"Dear Uncle Worst," said the letter. "You won't like this, but we are sending your great-nephew Warren for a short visit while we go skiing...."

The worst ran out onto the porch. "Stop!" he yelled. "Wrong address! This isn't for me! Return to sender!"
But the mail carrier was gone.

He read the rest of the letter. "We think Warren should meet his relatives, even you. We are enclosing some money for expenses. We will drop Warren off on Saturday, and pick him up on Sunday at 4:30. Try to be nice for once. Your nephew, Larry."

The worst went to the phone. "I want to make a collect call," he said, and gave the operator his nephew's number. There was a long wait.

"They won't accept the call," said the operator.

"Tell them it's their uncle," said the worst.

"They know that," said the operator.

The worst fed Daisy. Then he sat down and stared straight ahead. "This can't be happening," he said. "I detest relatives even more than regular people."

In the morning the worst's nephew, Larry, and Larry's wife, Bea, turned up.

"Hi, Uncle Worst," said Larry. "We haven't seen you in years!"

"I know that," said the worst.

"This is Warren, your great-nephew," said Bea.

"Small, aren't you?" said the worst.

"At least I don't look like an old mummy," said Warren.

"You'll have loads of fun together," said Larry.

"What makes you think so?" said the worst.

Larry and Bea said good-bye.

"I suppose you want to come in," said the worst.
"Wait for Arnold," said Warren. He gave a whistle.
"Who's Arnold?" said the worst.

"*He* is," said Warren as a huge dog marched past the worst.
"That beast is not coming into this house," said the worst.
"Stop him!"
Arnold went thundering up the stairs.

"I can't believe you actually live in this dump," said Warren. "When's lunch?"

"When I say so," said the worst.

"I'm having it now," said Warren.

Warren went into the kitchen. He opened the icebox and all the cabinets. There was hardly anything in them.

"What do you eat around here?" said Warren.

"Dried fruit," said the worst. "Dry cereal..."

"It figures," said Warren.

"Where's my room?" said Warren.
The worst led him upstairs.
"There," said the worst,
pointing.
"No way," said Warren.

Warren ran into the
worst's room and
bounced on the bed.
"*This* is my room!"
he said.

"It's *my* room," said the worst.
Arnold growled, and the worst stepped back.
"*Was* your room," said Warren.
"I'm a *guest*!"
Warren and Arnold ran downstairs.
"This is outrageous," said the worst.
"Utterly outrageous."

When the worst went downstairs, Warren was using the phone.
"What's the address here?" said Warren.
"121 East Forsythia," said the worst. "Why?"

"They wanted to know where to deliver the pizza," said Warren.
"Pizza? Deliver?" said the worst. "I will not allow it."
"Too late," said Warren.

When the pizza arrived, they sat down and ate in silence.
The worst said, "Never had pizza before."
"Like it?" said Warren.
"Not much," said the worst. "Who's going to clean up this mess?"

"Probably not Arnold and definitely not me," said Warren. "Who does that leave?"
They went out to play.
"That child is a monster," said the worst.

The worst tried to take a nap,
but snowballs kept
thudding against the house.

He opened the door,
and a volley of snowballs
flew into the living room.

Warren and a lot of
neighborhood children were
throwing snowballs.
"Stop that immediately,"
yelled the worst,
"or I will call 911!"

The worst again tried to take a nap. It was very quiet. He kept listening for sounds, but there weren't any. "What are they up to now?" he said.

Warren and the children were making a snowman. The neighbors stopped to watch. "Looks just like you, Mr. Worst!" they called. "Very good!"

The worst turned red. “Come inside this instant!” he cried.

A parade of children and dogs marched into the house. “Just Warren!” said the worst, but nobody heard him. One fat dog barked at Daisy, who took off like a shot and disappeared.

The children looked around. “Weird, huh?” said one of them.

“You think this is bad,” said Warren, “you should see the rest of the house!”

The children began running through the rooms, laughing and yelling.

The worst made his way up to the attic.
He closed the door and waited for everybody to leave.

The children slid down the stairs on pillows. They played hide-and-seek. They brought old toys up from the cellar. They tried on the worst's hats and galoshes. They built castles and airplanes out of the furniture and rugs.

Later some of them went home and brought back lots of snacks, and everybody had a feast.

At six in the morning the worst came down from the attic to look for Daisy. Warren and Arnold were asleep on his bed.

In the living room something crunched under his foot.
He reached for the light switch. It was sticky.
"Eegh!" said the worst.

The worst turned on the light. He was standing on a pile of broken cookies. The furniture was upside down. There were plates and glasses and chocolate everywhere and fudge footprints all around.

The kitchen was worse.

"Warren! Get down here this instant!" called the worst.

Warren and Arnold came down the stairs, yawning.

"Clean up this mess!" said the worst.

"Now?" said Warren. "No way."

"Immediately!" said the worst.

Then the worst went outside to search for Daisy.
He walked up and down the street, looking and calling.

When he got back, the house was clean.
"There!" said Warren. "Now the place looks just as ugly as usual."

Warren started up the stairs. Then he turned around. "I'm telling my parents how you made me work and clean your dumb house and stay in that room and have no breakfast," he said. "Then they'll know how horrible you are!"

"They already know that," said the worst. "Ha!"

"I guess you're right," said Warren.

"I'm going to tell your parents how you wrecked my house and scared my dog, Daisy, so much she ran away!" said the worst. "Ha!"

"Maybe Daisy didn't like being around you any more than we do!" said Warren. "Ha!"

The worst didn't answer, so Warren said "Ha!" again.

“Arnold could find Daisy for you if he wanted to,” said Warren.
“But you’d have to ask him nicely. You know—say ‘please.’ ”
“I don’t ask favors from dogs,” said the worst.
“Then he won’t find Daisy,” said Warren.

"P-p-p-," said the worst very softly.

"Louder!" said Warren.

"P-please," said the worst.

"Okay, Arnold," said Warren. "Find Daisy!"

Arnold raced through the house, sniffing.

He stopped in the parlor, his nose twitching.

He tiptoed up to the old Victrola.

Out peeked Daisy.

Arnold marched into the living room, carrying Daisy.
"Daisy!" cried the worst.
"Good boy, Arnold!" said Warren.

Arnold dropped Daisy on the floor in front of the worst.
She jumped up onto his lap.
The worst looked at Warren. “Ha,” he said.
“She likes you,” said Warren. “I don’t know why.”

The worst gave them dog bones—one for Daisy, three for Arnold.

When Bea and Larry drove up that afternoon, Bea said, "I can't believe it!"

The worst and Warren were making a big snowdog together.

Stockton Twp. Pub. Lib.
140 W. BENTON
STOCKTON, IL 61085

“Thanks for taking care of Warren,” said Larry to the worst.
“It wasn’t too bad, was it?”

“Yes, it was,” said the worst.

“Maybe another little visit next year?” said Bea.

“Don’t count on it,” said the worst.